The Stolen Car

The University of Massachusetts Press

Amherst, 1989

POEMS

The Stolen Car

JAMES HAUG

Why we stuck to the baby carriage I don't know.
It was unlikely other children would be born and
the wheels were broken. People who have few
possessions cling tightly to those they have. That
is one of the facts that make life so discouraging.
—Sherwood Anderson, "The Egg"

Nothing can equal in polish and obscured
origin that dark instrument

A car
—George Oppen, *Discrete Series*

CONTENTS

The Stolen Car

NIGHT SWIMMER

He took the rope out to the end
of its swing and let go,
knees tucked up to his chest.
The rope held, then gave way
like a signature going slack.
Vapor rose from the black
surface. He broke the surface,
eyes shut, the water of Bullhead
Pond warmer than the air,
and sprung open underwater.
The current pressing like slow wind,
he pushed down to touch the silt.
He found a tooth of metal,
an old bicycle, a shopping cart,
a Mercury with the keys still in it,
odd pieces of tubing wrenched
like a twisted alphabet, a washing
machine. And whatever it was then
that had him would not let him go.
He was becoming the mayor of a city
where no one lives,
where the only news is fish
and new additions. Was it crazy,
that architecture of chance, the clear
planets of his breath rising?
On the drowned streets where he took
his first black swallow,
he was learning the language.

one

TERMINAL HOTEL

There's always a vacancy here.
A doorman under the ragged canopy
wears his heart out, waiting
decades for a crimson Packard,
and rubs the eagle clean
off a silver dollar.
He's been witness to Prohibition,
the Red Scare, and urban renewal—
and now you, stepping down,
uncertain in the glare of departing
buses, the bag at your feet
caved in like a broken hat,
empty of everything you knew
you wouldn't need but the fake
beard and the i.d. of someone
who looks just like you.
It is midday. The sun fires
the color right out of your eyes,
sidewalk hot enough to fry.
You want lemonade, a good smoke.
You sit in the chair and rest
a foot on the metal step. A boy
bends over your shoe and applies
black polish, then the stained chamois.
In this kind of heat you realize
it could take forever: the boy
muttering over your wing tips,
the doorman's pocket full of change.

1951

When they got to that town in Korea,
the only thing left standing
was the brewery. My father
blew out his breath
when they found the place deserted
and pulled a louse from his beard.

The troops cracked the enormous vats
and shoved their helmets
into the stream until foam
spilled over the edges
and green beer ran down the street.

On the fourth day of drinking,
a soldier found an eye
gazing from the beer in his helmet
and fainted. They fished
thirteen bodies from the tanks.

And sailing home my father dealt
poker, high stakes, in the hold.
He drank the first night back.
He bought a Studebaker with cash.
At his new job, in the armory,
he passed my mother in a hallway;
they still had not met.

CLOUD RISES SEVEN MILES
FROM OBSERVERS

Think of the awful dark the sky gets
in 1953
over Yucca Flats, Nevada.
The television camera is secured
on the top of a utility truck
and a sound man tilts his head
toward the static of a distant relay
inside the cups of his headset.
All of us are waiting
for something big to go off,
a second dawn to bolt
straight up and redefine the horizon, bend
orbits, recast the universe
to the size of a dollhouse,
where we may examine corner to corner
the stress points, the extent of damage
we can sustain
before it falls down, a future
neat and angular, lit by a single bulb.

And over the next guy's shoulder you see
we're not that far, as if the ferry
will soon return to bear us
across the river, the bank first dim
and then bright enough
to pierce the thin door of an eyelid.
And there is no way to explain this morning,
a man thinks as he drives on to work:
how a perfect sun rose black in his eye,
how across the desert
a family sat down early to breakfast
as the windows shook above the sink,
and they lost no faith in the world turning,
with school lunches bagged and ready
and daylight coming for the kids.

KITTYHAWK

A current of sand
ran beneath your feet
as you lifted off.
The earth fell away
like your hometown,
waving then
turning its back.

You lay on the cool
palms of the wind,
dipping the wings
the way a hawk coasts
on a bank of air,
and squinted into
clouds, the future.

HEAT: A COMPOSITE, 1977

In front of the New York Public Library,
a man leaves a violet on a bench and enters
the crowd sleepwalking on lunch hour.
I am eating slowly from a brown paper bag.
Dressed in painter's whites, blue-smeared,
sweaty, I am keeping an eye on the clock.
Late last night, a young man and woman
were shot, parked beneath a busted streetlamp
in Brooklyn. A public outcry has arisen
for crime lights, composites. Stories circulate
of innocent men pursued, identities mistaken.
And the King's bloated face balloons
from the front page of the *Daily News*.
Through the bright window of a pizza joint
I see the shoulders of a woman shudder
as she weeps, pressing dough on a flat pan,
and I wonder if she mourns Graceland, if a man's
choosing something else on the jukebox.
Last night, when Son of Sam pulled the door
shut of his car, a command scratching
like an insect inside of his ear,
I was lying on a floor in Queens, a heat island
floating behind my eyes, half-dreaming
brush strokes of the sky on an endless wall,
marble stairs, blue narcotic petals.

Not a life you look inside of,
it all unravels out
the ear-dark bell. Close
your eyes. The red
shoes click down the hall, up
stairs to A sharp; a

web of perfume spins itself.
Your gloved hand parts
the curtain in a rented room
somewhere stories above
steam and a real city, a red
twitching of neon. Loss moves

across the hall, unpacking
its cardboard suitcase. Nothing
will disturb this long solo,
riffing off the dawn
that comes down like a fine
mist of disappointment:

the feathered brush of a street-
sweeper, the tiny report
of high heels outside the door,
the cold figure smoking, back
against a Buick, waiting for you
on the loneliest street in town.

I climb seven flights to the top.

On the fifth floor landing a woman
sets down a grocery sack, jerking
house keys through her fingers.
My heart, she says.

The only way to calm her
is to keep going.

The cabbie downstairs turns up
alive night after night,
singing to himself,
beating time on what's at hand.

I passed his open door once.
No furniture, just a radio playing
on the floor, the bare windows
dirty with sunlight.

When the sun climbs the glass faces
of skyscrapers,
a clarinet will run down the scale.
A vertical life.
The world goes to work without me.

Once I wanted to work construction:
high rise, flat-footed
on steel girders, lunch a half-mile up,
on the edge, and singing.

SONG FOR STOLEN BREAD

Here's the green delivery truck pulling away,
here's the black nest of fumes.
Hungry, awake before the birds,
we crawled out from an abandoned car,
from a lean-to or an all-night john,
through the hole in a chain-link fence
or a tunnel burrowed in thicket,
just two or three of us,
rubbing our bellies, wearing your clothes,
staking out the boxes the driver leaves
in front of the darkened grocer's.
We tore warm handfuls of the fresh bread
from the white sleeve, the white sleeve
glowing like linen in moonlight
between a brick wall and a dumpster.
This is a song for the worm ingesting the earth,
for the mad jay and his stale crust of bread,
rasping at first light,
when the big trucks gear down on 25:
King Kullen, Purity Supreme, Acme, Wonder.

MEETING WALTER

Breaking and entering,
Walter called what he did
the night before, and tipped
back the bottle of corn
whiskey in the cornfield.
This bottle he stole,
and some jewelry
which he threw in a sump.
Sumps, he slurred,
where the run-off gathers
and levels high by morning.
Sometimes they'd find
a small kid there belly down,
reading the bottom.
The bottle he launched
flared in the sun, and broke.
Down the hill behind
the outlet, we sent blown
retreads wobbling
across the busy turnpike
and put a stop to traffic.
His mother shut in at home he'd
avoid till he sobered,
even if it meant
sleeping in an empty lot.
Once, he said, he brought her,
skinny, to the carnival,
and he paid, and he
let the big wheel take her
around and around.
After such beginnings, I left him
passed out in that field.

DRY ICE

The man on a break
    at the ice plant
    takes down his battered

pea coat from the nail
    driven in the wall.
    He's pulling the graveyard

alone tonight
    and likes it that way,
    the rumbling cough when

the freezer kicks in
    and a tremor wrinkles
    the brown skin of sweet

coffee in his thermos.
    With tongs he enters
    a cooler, arctic

smoke blowing through
    the doorway, floating
    over blocks stacked

in the white icelight.
    He clamps a slab
    of dry ice, hefts it

out of the cooler
    and sets it upon
    the tin countertop,

a small blue window
    between now and the past,
    which he tries to see

not through but into:
    a blank sky one morning,
    the pond where he cut

out of school and swam
in the shade of a willow,
where the war never came,

where huge dozers
had come to rest
before the ice age.

THE LESSON

On the whetstone,
with a butcher's eye,
he ground the oiled
blade because
he liked a knife sharp.
Then he sent the girl
beside him to bring
a pan from the kitchen.
When she came back
he'd undone the ribbon,
his clean fingers
gone tender, cooing
in the lamb's ear.
I want you, he said,
to watch the pan,
keep it tilted, so.
He drew back the knife
as she knelt
and tipped the pan
in her hands
so she would hold on
just right and catch
and catch it all.

Below the rocker panel, my father
held out a hand, and clawed the air.
The cobbled red clouds darkened,
and I placed a boxwrench
cold as a star on his blackened palm.
"We're losing daylight," he called
under the chassis, a rusted bolt there
he could not reach. I laid my hand on
the smudged fender and bent down:
It's no good, nothing I can do.
He struggled against the frozen bolt,
his shoulder blades grinding
into the tar. I saw myself stretched
in the hubcap, *Ford* stitched across
my chest, then squirmed under with him
shining a flashlight. "It's no good,"
he breathed, and rested. The green anchor
from Korea blurred on his forearm.
The radio reported napalm. In 1970,
I was afraid of my father's veteran rage,
his death-haunted sleep would haunt me.
"The sky's red from factories," he said,
"ferric oxide maybe." Or maybe it was
the west burning down, New Jersey on fire,
gulls shot with iron, red hot
and wheeling fiercely, the angry ignition
of a spark touched to gasoline.
But he was back at the unyielding fact
of metal, pounding a flattened hand
against tempered steel, and the days
now grown so short. I crawled out
rubbing grit from an eye, and already
headlights were coming on. My father
grunted once more, and slid from under
as we disappeared. I watched my nails,

five black crescents orbiting the pale
globe of my hand, and followed the gradual
illumination of living rooms
down the block, foreign as other countries.
He wiped the bright wrenches one by one
and held them up against the sky,
the thin line of the sunset shutting out
another small world, and I wanted to leave
that beautiful, stupid country for good.

two

THE STOLEN CAR

In the parking lot a brand new Harley
won't cool down. Road dust spun
from a truck's tires billows, climbs
like heat, yellow dry, and ages
the moon. Brushing his pants, Walter
says he'll clean that guy's clock.
Clean means a lot, he spits,
but his boots have lost that shine.

Our other boots caked with clay
and stashed in the trunk will curl,
stiffen by morning when the crow
stirs and I count out the money left,
the miles. Walter says we live on
wheels, and sleep where we park.
Tonight we're drinking in our last
clean clothes, born out of state,

and I feel the heat of noon coming
off the parked cars, the asphalt,
the painted cinder block walls
of The Blue Goose, the woods back
beyond the streetlamp. Once
I swore I'd find some decent work.
Now I work each day by the map.
From the ditch along Route 23

a sleek cricket answers the dark.
And after a break, the great engine
of guitars starts up. Walter combs
his hair in the chrome of a rag-top,
saying we could jump it for laughs
—and I think so too, how with luck
we'd joyride back roads that ran out
really somewhere for a change,

breathing the illegal air, top down,
and follow the track of the full moon
and land blessed in broad daylight,
a new world stripped down before us.
I fumble black wires under the dash
as Walter cups his lighter,
swearing through his teeth, Come on
man, start this son of a bitch.

AFTERNOONS

Cigarette smoke rolls off
the ceiling,
                ghost
of the last few hours.

Afternoons drinking,

the rim of this valley's
the edge of the world.

Zero visibility in the rain,
small planes
                grounded,
stalled on the airstrip.
              And even when
the postman's sober

the mail comes late.

Men stamp wet feet
through the door,
                and bar-light
turns gold in a beer glass,
soft
      and persistent

like the mutter of rain
or the idle
talk of the unemployed.

POOL IS A GODLESS SPORT

I like the articulate crack
the cue ball makes
on impact, how it drops
what it's after and backspins back,
the chalk skids
on its bald surface, blue
and hard as water
or your eye, keen straight
down the line of the poolstick,
how the clogged air of lies
and smoke clears as you circle
the table, the next shot
plump on the rail, a duck.
You're on a roll, playing
collisions of intent and dumb luck.
We don't talk as I gather
a new game in the rack;
no one's put down quarters.
We could shoot hours here.
The bartender yawns and looks on,
pinball bangs a free ball.
We play off the angles, combinations,
the felt before each break
fresh as promise,
and let the rolling geometry
plot our next move.

CLEAR

Blue light of morning, I drive
the valley roads. At flood stage
a stream erodes its black banks.
Noon inches higher each day.
If I must start somewhere
make it here,
renting spaces, a room, a body,
a skull like the one I look out of,
rings of bone the color
of fear and paper, the bleached
white cloud drifting south.
I want to tell you something about air,
a blue sheet of glass, or light,
wind holding up a glider, the absent
place where music goes, distances,
places where the air's so thin you grow
faint, inhaling with panic
—the way what we don't see
can keep us going.

Whatever he did, he left in a hurry—
took nothing with him.
The front door's jammed wide open,
floorboards warp and rise.
Starlings creak in the eaves.
The whole house seems to sag
under its own weight.
By weather, by curious neighbors,
it's been ransacked too long.

Sunlight's useless here.
The damp claims it all.
A broken-armed record player
gives up mahogany veneer.
Stacked 78s have no labels.
Unmatched shoes sidestep
the heaps of threadbare
pants piled on the floor.
Wallpaper curls off the wall.
And paperbacks have split open
like pale hothouse flowers.

The path worn in the carpet
leads from room to room.
I touch the surfaces of things,
straighten the picture
like this and like this.
I try all of it on for size.

PASSING THROUGH BARRE

A small town at the end of autumn,
pickups weathered hubdeep in leaves,
a stock car raised on blocks
with a bunch of dried flowers
stuffed in the radiator,

the local dropouts lounging
on the steps of Town Hall (now closed,
black shutters scrubbed and sealed)

act a double feature
the soundtrack of which only
they can hear, cruel afternoons
on Friday, the cold coming back
colder, precise, badly usual,

quicker than the jackknife
you never see,

and the library across from the green,
closed too, with its three books
slowly cracking their fragile spines
on shelves
in the unvisited dark.

DRIVING AROUND,

absent, and looking for a place
to eat, even Texas hot dog
stands are friendly. I finger

the notches like knuckles
along the wheel, let the grip
slide through and spin.

When I think I am getting lost
I turn into a blind drive
and realize it's your place:

the tractor tire strung
from a limb, a deaf child
swinging it back and forth

like a black coin,
the center all gone.

three

EDGES

Near the rusted tracks of the abandoned depot,
Off the Wall waits for high school girls
to come down made-up and lighting Kents.
He lifts the mouth of a paper sack
to his thin lips, inhales model airplane dope
deep within his lungs until they fatten
into heavy wings, and he is rising.
He draws a broad hunting knife from his belt
and scrapes a thumb across the fine edge,
the haft an axis he angles around,
playing-out knife games: mumblety-peg
with a hapless kid going home, or stretch.
Then he settles in the shade of a dumpster
and pares his nails with a gravity knife,
the same that lands him upstate on manslaughter.
With more dope, the glue dream takes over,
thickens, clots his speech. He stumbles
across the tracks into a cornfield, the dry
stalks ticking about his ears like dice.
He is running his hands through the blonde
hair of the sun, making peace with the dust,
with the earth that will never let him go,
and he is a dark flower nodding
in back of his garbage truck. His bones collect
themselves in the shape of an ancient bird,
its ragged cry tearing his throat, his black
feathers gassed back and shiny as a Cadillac.

WHAT RICHARD THINKS

He thinks he lives in hell.
He thinks the entire
population of history is entering
him. He is
everyone's window of pain.
He is guilty of the murders
the television recounts
every night. He smokes three
packs a day and peels back
his eyelids, sleepless as ice.
Through him we see our suffering,
our ecstatic burning.
He thinks he is being fucked by God,
that the police are knocking for him
—the most radiant man on earth!
Now he is hiding
behind the laced bone-work
of his fingers, or out
naked on a fire-
escape that is brittle
and without a building.

GROUNDS

The way he folds his hands above
the coffee cup tells me it's a job
you perform without complaint.
He breaks a honey-glazed donut
over his napkin, fingernails rimmed
with loam, and chews a small piece
thoughtfully and bends to sip
the cup the waitress just refilled.
He slides two soiled quarters
beneath the saucer for a tip. Outside
the sun lifts itself burning
behind the doctors' homes of Chestnut
Hill, and he points out the trimmed
grass courts, frosted and spikey
as green glass; shows me the wilted
runs of lawn along the foul lines,
the service corners scuffed bald.
I haul out the sodcutter and shovels
and fight off the urge to sleep
or quit. He kneels down hunched
like a comma in last year's mulch
and tells me I'll get minimum
to start then cuts a square of earth
with a hand spade and firmly
tamps it in a hole just its size,
patting down the green quilting.
If he hates his life he won't let on.
He tells me, cut it large, make it
fit, and after one year a raise,
then turns back to cross the field.
I nudge a sod clump with my boot,

the morning frost becoming dew.
Somewhere the 7:12 commuter departs
as I bend to my new job and begin
the future, to make it fit,
and punch the ground all morning.

WHITE DUST

After the cement factory up the road
blankets her stoop with white dust,
the woman at the end of Mission Lane
brings out the frayed broom and works it
over the concrete steps, sending
dust bone-dry and contagious straight
to heaven. The small storms of dust
whiten the front door, her black shoes,
the doormat's welcome worn almost flat.
She wants things neat, but the vagrant dust
settles through the grid of power lines
and blanches skinny maples, a handful of sky,
plasters a whole new line of wash.
It lingers on the couch like a tired guest;
it flours a warm loaf of bread. One night

she watched her husband's immaculate ghost
drink glass after glass of water
in the kitchen until his eyes
turned dust and puffed out tiny clouds.
She wants no part of it, saving shirts limp
on wire hangers, hankies folded and rubbed thin,
used up on sweats and oil, on cold mornings,
the slow work by inches, the dust devils
whirling behind her when she walks away,
the dust committing its small violence
over the breakfast table as she tries
to make out news of the air. She leans

hard on the broom and gives dust
back to its maker, her anger raised
like the darkened knob of flesh
the broom stick chafes on her thumb.
The dust settles on the cramped earth
of her yard, a space large enough

to admit an hour of light or raise up
an entire man, where angels drag
each morning up white ladders of dust.

THE TREES IN MY PARENTS'
BACKYARD

One night in August
I learned to fly,
when cicadas chirred
along the dark
borders of the yard
and the smell of a late supper
idled up the dirt road
and I thought I might
like to change my name.
I had grown tired of it,
so tired I'd hand in
homework headed with my
dead grandfather's name.
That night I didn't want
to think of names
and watched instead the black
shadows of grown-ups
laughing to one another
and a small plane buzzing
mildly over my head.

When I heard my sister call
and another child hid
behind the forsythia,
frantic cries of delight
spreading over the yard,
I took off. I brushed
the tips of the crab apple
and sent a few ripe ones
thunking to the grass
and rose above the vacant shed
tangled in thicket,
tilted a little and circled

over my parents' house.
Blue jays were winging home
to drowse in a Norway
maple. The mimosa
lifted its fanlike limbs
on the least tug of a breeze,
and the generous aspen
shuddered and turned white.

The time Walter rolled the green
      Delta 88 on a switchback
  curve along Cove Road he called

me at three in the morning.
      He'd sideswiped a pole, leaving the Olds
  listing on its side, ditched,

and needed to explain how
      he entered that fourwheel drift. I was
  cranky with Walter, as always,

though glad to get out early
      Sunday morning and drive the Island,
  with nothing left to bless us

but the stark hour. I drove out,
      found him on a street corner, unhurt,
  smoking in a pay phone's light,

so we took turns at the wheel,
      the skin over Walter's knuckles raw
  and cracked from sanding bodywork

weekdays at Kenny's Auto.
      Headed east, we hauled along empty
  streets town after town, only

a few cruisers and gypsy
      cabs left, and the stoplights changing
  insensibly for no one.

On a good stretch down one main
      drag, we gunned it, catching green lights
  way out past the end of town,

then took the black roads edged by
      milkweed and sumac, past the sand pits
  scooped out of the low hills,

the summer homes now shuttered,
        the steeple behind a miniature
golf course, a vacant drive-in

sprawling beside a salt marsh.
        At that late hour we took in the real
life of things, how the world looks

when no one's looking at it.
        I'm not sure what came next: if we rolled
quietly by his girlfriend's,

and he whispered her a tale,
        or if we circled back the other way
past the shining Lilco stacks

and wound up at Sand City—
        the jetty where a concrete turret
stood crumbling on the gentler

side of the inlet, where fathers
        brought their kids to fish for eel, where
runaways and lovers slept

on the beach. Maybe we crouched
        there on the edge of Long Island,
knowing it could all wash away,

our backs turned on that dim world
        the world of men constructed for us,
the small surf breaking, drawing

back from shore, each wave dragging
        sand and old mortar into the Sound,
and Walter, sifting the sand,

said there's always other cars
        and marveled at how fast the sky pales,
how accidents brought us that far.

THE TENNESSEE WALTZ

He bows because he is nobody,
corrects the street
under its tilted little caps
of lamplight, and sets off again.
He sleeps near the railyards
where all night
the police come down
and trouble the stars,
club the soles of his feet,
move on, move on,
where the big engines bear down
at dawn
and rock the earth.
Too goddamn early, he swears,
when the hammers of morning
open a door in the sky.

At the Red Cross, they won't buy
blood like his. And why not
he wants to know,
the pint of Night Train
tucked in his back pocket,
and turns to the others waiting
in that room, his face
flushed dark as a bruise.
Night Train, he claims,
makes the blood red, see,
and under his thumb
bulges the thick green cords
of veins in his wrist.
But the nurse at her station
behind the sliding glass
won't have it, and tells him,
Come back when you're dry.

He turns and opens his arms,
cracks a stained grin
and enfolds the imaginary
body of a woman
in his careful, mute waltz.
The pint nearly empty,
he slumps into a folding chair
and rehearses the look of the world,
sober and meaningful
and quietly disengaged
from himself,
until he almost has it right,
the look of a man who waits
for a train
that will awaken the whole world.